THE AMERICAN G

17 64

KAYA, an adventurous Nez Perce girl whose deep love
for horses and respect for nature nourish her spirit

17 74

FELICITY, a spunky, spritely colonial girl,
full of energy and independence

18 24

JOSEFINA, an Hispanic girl whose heart and
hopes are as big as the New Mexico sky

18  54

KIRSTEN, a pioneer girl of strength and
spirit who settles on the frontier

18  64

ADDY, a courageous girl determined to be
free in the midst of the Civil War

19  04

SAMANTHA, a bright Victorian beauty, an
orphan raised by her wealthy grandmother

19  34

KIT, a clever, resourceful girl facing the
Great Depression with spirit and determination

19 44

MOLLY, who schemes and dreams on the
home front during World War Two

1934
CHANGES
FOR KIT
A Winter Story

By VALERIE TRIPP

ILLUSTRATIONS WALTER RANE

VIGNETTES SUSAN MCALILEY

American Girl®

Visit our Web site at **americangirl.com**

Printed in China.
03 04 05 06 07 08 LEO 12 11 10 9 8 7 6

The American Girls Collection®, Kit®, Kit Kittredge®, and American Girl®
are registered trademarks of Pleasant Company.

PICTURE CREDITS
The following individuals and organizations have generously given
permission to reprint images contained in "Looking Back":
pp. 60–61—Photograph Copyright © 2001: Whitney Museum of American Art
(*Employment Agency*, by Isaac Soyer); Library of Congress, LC-USF33-012949-M1 (sweeping girls);
© Underwood & Underwood/CORBIS (bank line); Franklin D. Roosevelt Library (FDR);
pp. 62–63—© Bettmann/CORBIS (suntanned starlets, NRA poster, WPA mural painter);
© CORBIS (women painters poster); National Archives Photo No. 69-N-2284 (puppet maker);
Library of Congress (cartoon); pp. 64–65—© Bettmann/CORBIS (Eleanor Roosevelt in coal mine);
© CORBIS (three children and coats); Franklin D. Roosevelt Library (dust storm);
Library of Congress LC-USF34-016459-E (migrant girl with baby);
pp. 66–67—Hugo Jaeger/TimePix (Hitler); © Hulton-Deutsch Collection/CORBIS
(munitions workers); © Bettmann/CORBIS (Pearl Harbor attack, war correspondent);
© Bettmann/CORBIS (*New York Journal*); © Francis G. Mayer/CORBIS (*New York Times*);
printed by permission of the Norman Rockwell Family Trust, © 1943 Norman Rockwell
Family Trust/CORBIS (*Freedom from Want*, by Norman Rockwell).

Cover Background Illustration by Paul Bachem

Library of Congress Cataloging-in-Publication Data

Tripp, Valerie, 1951–
Changes for Kit : a winter story / by Valerie Tripp ;
illustrations, Walter Rane ; vignettes, Susan McAliley.

p. cm. — (The American girls collection)
Summary: In 1934, during the Depression, Kit's cantankerous uncle comes
to live in the Cincinnati boardinghouse run by her parents, enlisting her aid
in transcribing his complaining letters to the editor of the local newspaper,
and inspiring her to write a different kind of letter of her own.
ISBN 1-58485-027-2 (hc.). — ISBN 1-58485-026-4 (pbk.)
1. Depressions—1929—Juvenile fiction.
[1. Depressions—1929—Fiction. 2. Authorship—Fiction. 3. Boardinghouses—Fiction.
4. Uncles—Fiction. 5. Conduct of life—Fiction. 6. Cincinnati (Ohio)—Fiction.]
I. Rane, Walter, ill. II. McAliley, Susan, ill. III. Title. IV. Series.
PZ7.T7363 Cgh 2001 [Fic]—dc21 2001021312

FOR MY MOTHER, KATHLEEN MARTIN TRIPP,
WHO INSPIRED BOTH KIT AND ME, WITH
LOVE AND THANKS

TABLE OF CONTENTS

KIT'S FAMILY
AND FRIENDS

DAD
*Kit's father, a
businessman facing
the problems of the
Great Depression.*

MOTHER
*Kit's mother, who takes
care of her family and
their home with strength
and determination.*

KIT
*A clever, resourceful
girl who helps her family
cope with the dark days
of the Depression.*

CHARLIE
*Kit's affectionate
and supportive
older brother.*

UNCLE
HENDRICK
*Mother's wealthy and
disapproving uncle.*

MRS. HOWARD
Mother's garden club friend, who is a guest in the Kittredge home.

STIRLING HOWARD
Mrs. Howard's son, whose delicate health hides surprising strengths.

RUTHIE SMITHENS
Kit's best friend, who is loyal, understanding, and generous.

SOMETHING WONDERFUL

Something wonderful was going to happen. Kit Kittredge knew it the minute she and her friends Ruthie and Stirling walked in the door after school.

Mother was waiting for them in the front hall. "Here you are at last," she said, sounding cheerfully impatient. "Hang up your coats. Then come join me in the living room."

Mother left, and Kit turned to Ruthie and Stirling. "I wonder what's up," she whispered.

Ruthie shrugged and Stirling said, "Who knows?" But Kit saw them slip sly smiles to each other, so she knew they were in cahoots with Mother.

The children hurriedly hung up their coats, took off their boots, and rushed into the living room. Stirling's mother, Mrs. Howard, was there looking happy and fluttery. Kit's older brother, Charlie, had a smile a mile wide. Miss Hart and Miss Finney, two nurses who were boarders in the Kittredges' house, simply beamed. Even Grace, Kit's dog, wore a goofy, drooly, doggy grin. But no one looked happier than Mother as she came toward Kit.

"This is for you, dear," Mother said. She was holding a winter coat. It was made of dark gray wool tweed flecked with blue. It had deep pockets and cuffs, four big buttons, and a belt.

"Wow," breathed Kit.

"Try it on!" said Ruthie. "See how it fits."

"Yes," insisted everyone. "Go ahead."

Kit hesitated. "It's a beautiful coat," she said. "I really like it. But . . ."

Kit knew her family didn't have a penny to spare. Her father had lost his business almost a year and a half ago because of the Depression. Ever since then, they'd had to struggle to pay the mortgage on their house every month. Kit asked, "Isn't a new coat like this awfully expensive?"

2

Much to Kit's surprise, everyone laughed.

"This coat isn't new," said Mother. "It belonged to Dad."

Mrs. Howard piped up. "Your mother and I took his old coat apart, washed the material, cut it to size, and made a new coat for you using the material inside out," she said proudly. "Wasn't that clever of us?"

"It sure was," agreed Kit, who believed that her mother was the cleverest mother in the world. It had been Mother's idea to turn their home into a boarding house. She had made a go of it in spite of hard times and the disapproval of her rich, grumpy old Uncle Hendrick, who was sure it would be a disaster. There were five boarders now: Miss Hart and Miss Finney, a musician named Mr. Peck, and Stirling and his mother. Aunt Millie and the Bells had left. The rent the boarders paid helped the Kittredges make ends meet, though they still had to be very thrifty. Kit grinned. "I like the coat even more knowing that it's not exactly new," she said.

"Good," said Miss Hart. "Then you'll like our surprise, too." She winked at Miss Finney and Ruthie.

"Ta da!" sang Miss Finney. She and Ruthie presented Kit with a knitted red hat and blue-and-red mittens.

"These aren't exactly new, either," Ruthie said. "The red yarn came from an old sweater of Stirling's that we unraveled, and the blue yarn came from a cap of Charlie's that Grace chewed."

"Unfortunately, Grace and I have the same taste in caps," said Charlie. He crossed his arms over his chest and pretended to frown down at Grace. But Grace, far from looking ashamed, seemed pleased with herself for her part in the creation of the mittens. She thumped her tail importantly.

"Go on, Kit," said Ruthie. "We're dying to see how everything looks."

Mother held the coat as Kit slipped her arms into the sleeves. Then Kit buttoned the buttons, buckled the belt, and pulled on the mittens and the hat.

"The hat goes like this," said Mother, tilting Kit's hat *just so*. "There," she said. "Perfect. Now turn around so we can see the whole effect."

Kit spun around. Charlie whistled, Stirling clapped, and all the ladies *oohed* and *aahed*. Kit blushed. She felt a little bashful about being the center of attention. But she knew that everyone was glad to have an excuse to make a happy fuss. Back before the Depression began, when her family had plenty of money, no one would have carried on much about a new coat. Now it was something to celebrate.

"Oh, look!" said Mrs. Howard. "Everything fits like a dream."

"And it's so stylish!" added Miss Finney.

"The coat makes you look really tall, Kit," said Ruthie with an approving air. "The whole outfit is very grown-up."

"I love it," Kit said. "Thank you, every one of you. It's wonderful. All of it." Kit held the collar to her nose and took a deep, delicious breath of the clean-smelling, woolly material. She felt warm and cozy, all the more so because the coat and hat and mittens had been made for her by her friends and family out of things that had belonged to them. It was as if affection had been sewn into the seams of the stout wool coat and knitted into the hat and mittens to cover Kit with warmth from head to toe. She sighed a sigh of pure pleasure. "It was very nice of all of you to make these things for me," she said.

"Well, you desperately needed a new coat," said Mother. "Your old coat has been too small for two years now."

Kit had a sudden thought. "Mother," she asked, "do we need my old coat? Are you planning to take it apart and make something out of *it*, too?"

"Why, no," answered Mother. "I don't think so."

"Then may I give it away?" asked Kit. She explained, "I keep thinking about the children Stirling and I saw in the hobo jungle last summer. This cold weather must be terrible for them." The summer before, Kit and Stirling had gone to the hobo jungle, which was the place by the railroad tracks where hoboes camped. Kit had been surprised and saddened to see a whole family there, with little children. Many times since then she'd wished she could do something for those hobo children. Their shoes were so worn out and their clothes were so thin and ragged! Now she asked Mother, "Would it be all right if Stirling and Ruthie and I went to the jungle this afternoon? Maybe there's a girl there who could use my old coat."

"I think that's a very good idea," said Mother.

She turned to Mrs. Howard and asked, "Is it all right with you if Stirling goes, too?"

Mrs. Howard nodded. "As long as they stay away from the trains," she said, "and come home before dark."

"We'll be back in time to do our chores before dinner," Kit promised.

"Hurry along, then," said Mother. "And Ruthie, be sure to stop by your house and ask your mother for permission to go."

"I will!" said Ruthie.

Kit folded her old coat over her arm as Ruthie and Stirling put their coats and boots back on. Then the children went outside, bundled up against the February afternoon. Kit smiled. She hardly felt the cold, snug as she was in her not-exactly-new, wonderful winter coat, hat, and mittens!

Ruthie's mother gave Ruthie permission to go. She also gave the children a sack of potatoes for the hoboes. The children took turns carrying the sack as they walked through town and past the front of Union Station. Kit was sure of the way. But when they came to the spot next to the river where the hobo jungle had been during the summer, it was deserted.

"Where'd the jungle go?" asked Stirling.

"Are you sure we're in the right place?" asked Ruthie.

Kit looked around. Not one tired hobo was lying asleep on the ground with his hat over his face, or resting his weary feet, or repairing his travel-worn shoes. There were no tents or rickety lean-tos propped against the trees, no hungry children eating stew, no clothes spread on the bushes to dry as there'd been in the summer. There was no fire inside the circle of stones on the windswept, bare ground, no scent of coffee, no music. All was oddly quiet.

"Hey," said Stirling. "Look."

He pointed, and Kit and Ruthie saw smoke rising up, dark gray like a pencil squiggle against the pale winter sky. The smoke was coming straight out of the ground! Kit looked more closely and saw that someone had dug a cavelike shelter into the embankment under the bridge. There was even a door built into the hillside.

"Come on," Kit said. She knocked on the door.

A man with a weather-beaten face opened it. "Yes?" he asked. His gruff voice reminded Kit of stern Uncle Hendrick.

"Excuse me, sir," Kit said politely. "But where are all the hoboes?"

"Someplace south, if they're smart," said the man. "There are five of us living in this cave and we don't have room for any more."

"But what about the ones who are riding the rails?" asked Kit. "Lots of people camped here last summer when they were passing through town."

"Humph!" harrumphed the man. "Don't you know that this is Cincinnati's coldest winter in twenty-nine years? Folks'd freeze to death camping out. Most hoboes who are passing through go to soup kitchens or missions. Sometimes they can stay for a night or two if they do chores. Then they have to move on."

"Oh, I see," said Kit. She thanked the man, and Ruthie gave him the sack of potatoes. Then Kit, Stirling, and Ruthie walked to the soup kitchen on River Street. They'd once delivered a Thanksgiving basket of food there, so they knew to go to the back

9

door to make their delivery. They went inside and carefully made their way past the stoves steaming with pots of soup, around the busy people making sandwiches and coffee, and through the swinging door to the front part of the soup kitchen where the food was served.

The three children stopped still and stared at the crowded room. An endless line of men, women, and children shuffled in the front door and past the tables where soup, bread, and coffee were served. Every seat at every table was taken, so many people had to eat standing up. Groups of people, grim and gray, were gathered in the corners. Families huddled together wherever they could and spoke in low murmurs. Somewhere a baby was crying. *So many people,* thought Kit sadly, *young and old, and all so hungry and poor.*

Kit knew that only luck and chance separated her family from those she saw around her. Almost two years ago her own father had come to this very soup kitchen to get food for her family because he had run out of money. That year they fell so far behind in paying the mortgage that they would have been evicted—thrown out of their house—if Dad's

So many people, thought Kit sadly, young and old,
and all so hungry and poor.

Aunt Millie had not rescued them with her life savings. Things were better for Kit's family now. But the Depression had taught Kit that nothing was certain. Everything could change suddenly, and she could find herself standing in line for soup, just like these children.

It made Kit's heart hurt to see them. One child was wearing a filthy, worn-out, threadbare coat that was much too small. Another wore a ragged overcoat that dragged on the ground. One even wore a blanket tied around his waist with rope. Their shoes were even worse. Some of the children had nothing but rags wrapped around their feet. Others wore broken-down boots with no laces, rubber galoshes they'd lined with old newspapers, or too-small shoes with the front part cut so that their toes poked out.

Ruthie tugged on Kit's sleeve. She nodded her head toward an area where people were sitting on the floor, leaning against the wall. "There's someone who needs your coat," she said.

At first, all Kit could see was what looked like a pile of dirty rags. But then she saw a little girl's thin, pinched face above the rags, and she realized that the rags were the little girl's skimpy coat—or what was left of it. It was badly stained and torn. The pockets had been ripped off and used to patch the elbows, and all the buttons but one were gone. The little girl was cuddled up to her mother. Her hair was tangled, her eyes were dull, and she seemed as lifeless and colorless as a shadow.

Kit, Ruthie, and Stirling went over and quietly stood in front of the girl and her mother. Kit held out her old coat. "Ma'am," she said to the mother, "may I give this coat to your little girl?"

The woman didn't answer. She looked at Kit as if she didn't quite believe what she had heard. But the little girl stood up. Shyly, eagerly, she took the coat from Kit and put it on over her ragged one. She smoothed the front of the coat with both hands, and then she raised her face to Kit. In that moment, something wonderful happened. The little girl was transformed from a ghost to a real girl. She hugged herself, and her pale cheeks glowed. "Thank you," she said to Kit, smiling a smile that lit her whole face.

Kit smiled back. "You're very welcome," she said. She could tell that the little girl felt the same way *she* had felt about *her* new coat. It warmed her both inside and out.

Bright, brilliant streaks of pink and purple were splashed across the late-afternoon sky as Kit, Ruthie, and Stirling walked home from the soup kitchen.

"Kit, you were like the fairy godmother who turned Cinderella's rags into a ball gown," said Ruthie, who liked fairy tales. "You gave that girl your old coat and *whoosh*." She waved an imaginary wand. "You changed her."

"Maybe," said Kit. "But that was just one coat and just one kid. Every kid there needed a coat— and shoes."

"Those poor kids," said Ruthie, "having to sleep on the floor! It's terrible that there's no better place for them to stay. Isn't there *anywhere* their parents could look for help?"

"I think," said Stirling, "they *are* looking for help. That's why they're on the road. Maybe they heard about jobs in New York or California. Or maybe they ran out of money and lost their homes, so they're traveling to friends or family, hoping to be taken in. They don't have any money for train fare, so they have to ride the rails. They can't pay for a hotel, so they eat and sleep at soup kitchens for a day or two. Then they're on their way again."

"In the freezing cold," added Kit. "In their ragged coats and worn-out shoes." She sighed. If only she had a hundred coats to give away, and a hundred pairs of shoes. *That* would be wonderful.

Kit and Stirling said good-bye to Ruthie at the end of her driveway and arrived home just as dusk fell. Kit went straight to work doing her evening chores. As she fed the dog and the chickens, scrubbed potatoes, and set the table for dinner, she remembered the hobo in his cheerless cave and the people in the crowded soup kitchen. *How lucky I am*, she thought. Her house might not be fancy. In fact, it was getting rather shabby. But it was warm and filled with good-hearted people who cared for one another.

Dinner was jolly that night. Afterward, Mr. Peck played his bass fiddle and Charlie played the piano. They made "Music to Do the Dishes By," and everyone sang along. Mother never used to allow the boarders to help clean up, but she had relaxed a bit

and treated them more like family now. Stirling
and Mrs. Howard sang as they cleared the table.
Miss Hart and Miss Finney chimed in as they helped
Mother wash the dishes. And Dad and Kit sang in
harmony as they dried. Grace, who never liked to be
left out, howled.

They were making so much noise that they
didn't hear Mr. Smithens, Ruthie's father, knocking
on the front door. They were surprised when he
stepped into the kitchen.

"Excuse me, folks," Mr. Smithens said. "I'm
sorry to barge in. But we had a call for you on our

telephone." The Kittredges could not afford a telephone, so the Smithenses kindly took calls for them. "It was Cincinnati Hospital," Mr. Smithens said to Mother and Dad. "It seems that your Uncle Hendrick had a fall and broke his ankle and his wrist. They've patched him up, and he's fine. But the nurse said he's making quite a ruckus. He wants you to come immediately and pick him up and bring him back here so that you can care for him until he's back on his feet. I'll drive you to the hospital as soon as you're ready to go."

"Thank you, Stan," said Dad. "We'll be right with you."

Mother had already taken off her apron and put on her hat and coat. In a minute, she and Dad were gone. The door closed behind them, and Kit stood in the sudden silence in the chilly front hall. *Oh no,* she thought, her heart sinking lower and lower as the news sank in. *Cranky, crabby, cantankerous Uncle Hendrick is coming to stay in our house. It'll be terrible.*

CHAPTER TWO

TO DO

"We've got to think of *something* to write," said Kit.

It was Saturday morning, and Kit, Ruthie, and Stirling were up in Kit's attic room, sitting around her typewriter. They were working on a newspaper. Before the Depression, Kit used to make newspapers for her father to tell him what had happened at home while he was away at work all day. Now that her family took in boarders, Kit made newspapers so that everyone in the household knew what was going on. When new boarders arrived, Kit always made a special newspaper to welcome them and to introduce them to the other boarders.

Usually, Kit's head was so full of things to write that her fingers couldn't move fast enough on the typewriter keys to keep up. In this case, however, the new boarders were Uncle Hendrick and his stinky dog, Inky. They'd been living with the Kittredges for more than a week, and so far, they had not endeared themselves to anyone. Even Grace, who liked *everybody* and lavished slobbery affection on complete strangers, kept her distance from Inky and showed a cool indifference to Uncle Hendrick. Kit couldn't think of anything to write about them that was both enthusiastic and honest.

"You could take a photograph of Uncle Hendrick," suggested Stirling. Kit had an old camera that her brother, Charlie, had fixed for her, and she was eager to use it. "A picture tells more about a person than words ever could."

"Maybe, but it costs money to get the film developed," said Kit, "so I was kind of hoping to take pictures of things I really liked."

"How about a drawing?" said Ruthie. "You're a good artist, Stirling. You could draw a picture of Uncle Hendrick."

19

"And Inky, too," added Kit.

"All right," said Stirling, opening up his sketch-pad. "Under my drawing I'll write, 'His bark is worse than his bite.'"

"Whose?" asked Ruthie, looking impish. "Inky's or Uncle Hendrick's?"

Kit smiled weakly at Ruthie's joke. Personally, she thought Uncle Hendrick's biting remarks were just as bad as the orders he barked at her.

Caring for Uncle Hendrick had turned out to be Kit's job. Mother was much too busy, and Dad had a part-time job at the airport. Charlie helped out while Kit was at school. But when she was home, Uncle Hendrick and Inky were her responsibility, and they were a big one.

Uncle Hendrick said he couldn't go up and down the stairs because of his ankle. Before school, Kit had to bring him his morning newspaper and his breakfast tray. She also had to walk Inky. Uncle Hendrick dozed all day, so when Kit came home from school, he was fully awake, full of pepper and vinegar, and full of demands and commands. He always made a big To Do list for Kit. Then he made a big speech about how to do everything on the To Do list. Then he made a big to-do about how she had done everything wrong on yesterday's To Do list.

And tasks and errands were not all. Uncle Hendrick grew bored sitting in his room with no one but Inky for company. He expected Kit to entertain him. During the first few days, Charlie had helped by playing checkers with Uncle Hendrick. But Charlie had won too often, and now Uncle Hendrick didn't want to play checkers with him anymore. He preferred badgering Kit. His idea of a conversation was to snap at her, "What's the capital of Maine?" or, "How much is seven percent of three hundred ninety two?" Having Uncle Hendrick in the house was every bit as terrible as Kit had thought it would be.

"Let's just write in our newspaper that we're sorry Uncle Hendrick hurt his ankle and his wrist, and we hope he is better soon," said Stirling.

"That's good," said Kit. She swiveled her chair around to face the desk and began *clickety-clacking* away on her old black typewriter. "And it's true, because the sooner he's better, the sooner he and Inky can go home!"

"The headline could be, 'The Sooner, The Better!'" joked Ruthie.

Suddenly, *bang, bang, bang!* A thunderous thumping shook the floor under the children's feet. It was accompanied by ferocious barking.

"Yikes!" said Ruthie, covering her ears. "What's *that?*"

"That's Uncle Hendrick calling me," said Kit. "He whacks his ceiling with his cane and then Inky barks. I'd better go see what they want."

"Go!" said Ruthie. "Stirling and I will finish up the newspaper."

"Thanks," said Kit. She gave up her chair to Ruthie, then pelted down the stairs and poked her head into Uncle Hendrick's room. "Do you need me, Uncle Hendrick?" she asked, shouting to be heard.

Uncle Hendrick stopped walloping the ceiling. Inky stopped barking, but threw in a few extra yips and growls for good measure. "What on earth was that infernal racket coming from upstairs?" asked Uncle Hendrick crossly.

"The headline could be, 'The Sooner, The Better!'" joked Ruthie.

Privately, Kit thought that Uncle Hendrick and Inky were the ones who'd made the racket. But she answered politely, "I was typing. Ruthie and Stirling and I are making a newspaper."

"What a waste of time," Uncle Hendrick snorted. "Making a pretend newspaper. Writing nonsense! Haven't you outgrown such silly childishness?"

Kit lifted her chin. She was rather proud of her newspapers. She never wrote nonsense. She loved writing, respected words, and tried hard to find the perfect ones to use, which was not the least bit childish to do. Now, for example, the perfect word to describe how she felt would be *annoyed*.

But Uncle Hendrick didn't notice her annoyance. As usual, he was concerned only about what he wanted. "Sit down!" he ordered. "I'll give you something worthwhile to write. Take a letter!"

Uncle Hendrick had broken the wrist on his right hand—his writing hand—so when he wanted to send a letter, he had to dictate it to Kit. Sometimes Kit thought that Uncle Hendrick had named his dog "Inky" because ink was something he liked to use so much. Almost every day, Uncle Hendrick dictated a letter. Usually it was a letter to the editor of the newspaper. And usually it was about "that man in the White House," which was what Uncle Hendrick called President Franklin Delano Roosevelt. Uncle Hendrick did not approve of FDR, which was what most people called the president. He did not like FDR's wife, Eleanor, either. As far as he was concerned, everything that was wrong with the country was their fault. Today Uncle Hendrick's angry letter was in response to a newspaper article he'd read about the programs FDR had started as part of the National Recovery Administration to fight the Depression.

President and Mrs. Roosevelt

"To the Editor," Uncle Hendrick began as soon as Kit was seated with pen and paper. "The NRA is a waste of taxpayers' money. It creates useless, make-work jobs so the government can hand out money to lazy idlers. FDR is drowning the USA in his alphabet soup of NRA programs, such as the CCC and the CWA."

Kit shifted in her chair. Uncle Hendrick knew perfectly well that last year Charlie had worked

for the CCC, or Civilian Conservation Corps, in
Montana for six months. Every month, Charlie
had sent home twenty-five of the thirty dollars he
earned. Her family had depended on it. Charlie
liked his experience in the CCC so much that he
hoped to sign up again. Uncle Hendrick also knew
that the Civil Works Administration, or CWA, had
given Dad the first job he'd had in almost two years.
It was just a short-term, part-time, low-paying job
clearing land and building stone walls out at the
airport. But Dad was glad to be working again. Kit
loved seeing him go off to work, whistling and
cheerful. He was proud of his work, and he thought
it might lead to a better job that would use his skills
as a mechanic. The other day at the hangar he'd met
an old friend named Mr. Hesse who'd said that soon
there might be work repairing airplane engines.

Kit pressed her lips together as Uncle Hendrick
went on saying critical things about the very
programs that were helping her family. "In short,"
Uncle Hendrick wound up, "when I say 'that man
in the White House' is going to be the ruination of
our fine country, all must agree."

I don't, thought Kit. But she kept her opinion to

herself. She had learned that it was useless to argue with Uncle Hendrick. It was best to concentrate on keeping up with him and writing exactly what he said without misspelling any words. If the letter was not perfect, Uncle Hendrick pounced on the mistakes and ordered Kit to copy the whole thing over again. He was a stickler.

Kit handed him the letter. He read it, gave a curt nod of approval, then took the pen and signed it as well as he could with his hand in a cast. "They don't print unsigned letters," he said. "Now, deliver this to Mr. Gibson at the newspaper offices immediately. No lollygagging!"

"Yes, sir," said Kit. Uncle Hendrick always acted as if the newspaper editor was waiting breathlessly for his letter and couldn't send the newspaper to press without it. He was absolutely confident that his letter would be printed. And rightly so, it seemed, because many of his letters did appear in the newspaper. Kit thought it was because he was rich and important. But she had to admit that though she disagreed with what he said, she admired how he said it. Uncle Hendrick expressed his opinions forcefully. He never wasted a word. He said precisely what he meant, with lots of vim and vigor.

Ruthie had left, and Stirling was busy drawing a picture of Kit in her new coat for their newspaper. So Kit went off on her errand alone. She knew the way well: down the hill, past the beautiful fountain in the center of the city, over two blocks and up one. The newspaper offices were not far from the soup kitchen. Kit saw lots of children in ragged coats and pitiful shoes, but not the little girl to whom she had given her coat. She hoped the girl and her mother were home, or at least someplace safe and warm and comfortable.

Kit smiled as she went inside the big brick building that housed the newspaper offices. She climbed the stairs briskly, her footsteps *tsk-tsking* as she did. She could just imagine how Uncle Hendrick would  *tsk-tsk* and sniff disdainfully if he knew how she loved to pretend that she was a reporter who worked in this building. She pushed open the door to the newsroom and was greeted with the clamor of telephones ringing, typewriters clacking, and people chatting. The noisy newsroom seemed like heaven to

Kit. *This is where the newspaper is created,* she thought.
*Stories that thousands of people will read are being
written right here, right now.*

As she walked through the room to Mr. Gibson's
desk, several people nodded to her. She'd delivered
letters to the newspaper offices so many times that
her face was familiar. Some of the friendlier reporters
even knew her name. "Hi, Kit," one said as she
passed by. "Got another letter for Gibb?"

"Yes, I do," Kit said. She knew they all called
Mr. Gibson, the editor, "Gibb."

Gibb was not very friendly. He sat frowning

behind his messy, cluttered desk. When Kit came near, he said without enthusiasm, "Put it in the box." He never even looked up.

"Yes, sir," said Kit. She put Uncle Hendrick's letter in Gibb's in-box on top of lots of other letters and a few rolls of film. Then she turned to go.

Kit wished she could linger in the newsroom. How she'd love to talk to the reporters! But she knew she had better hurry home to her chores. Saturday was the day she always washed all the sheets and put fresh ones on the boarders' beds. It also was the day she and Stirling went around the neighborhood selling eggs. After that, it would be time to help Mother with dinner. Kit was proud of the way she did her chores these days with great efficiency. *I bet I can find time to put the finishing touches on our newspaper,* she thought, *unless Uncle Hendrick has thought up something else for me to do.*

LETTERS WITH AN 'S'

On the last Sunday in February, Kit was trotting past the door to Uncle Hendrick's room with a laundry basket full of her clean clothes propped on her hip when she heard Uncle Hendrick call her.

"Kit, come here!" he barked. Inky barked, too, then followed up with a wheezy whine.

Kit stuck her head in the door. "Yes, sir?" she asked.

"Take a letter!" said Uncle Hendrick.

Not now! Kit thought. She'd been rushing to finish her chores ever since going out in the eerie early-morning light to get Uncle Hendrick's newspaper. Today was a special day. After lunch, Dad's

31

friend Mr. Hesse was going to drive Dad and Kit and Charlie to the airport. Kit had already carefully put her camera in her coat pocket because she wanted to photograph Dad standing next to some of the stone walls he'd built. She also hoped Charlie would take *her* picture posed next to an airplane, just like her heroine, the pilot Amelia Earhart. Mother had said that Kit could use some of the egg money to have the film developed.

Reluctantly, Kit lowered the laundry basket, entered Uncle Hendrick's room, and picked up the pen and paper. She hoped the letter would be short.

"Start by writing, 'To the Editor,'" Uncle Hendrick instructed Kit, precisely as he had done many times before. Then he cleared his throat and dictated, "This morning I read on page twenty-five of your newspaper that an empty hospital in Covington, across the river from Cincinnati, may be used as a home for transients and unemployed persons."

Kit looked up. "Really?" she asked. "What a great idea!"

"Quiet!" growled Uncle Hendrick, echoed by Inky. Uncle Hendrick went on dictating, "This is an outrage! Such a home will attract tramps and drifters from all over the country. They'll flock here to be housed, fed, and clothed at our expense. We'll be pampering worthless riffraff. All of these hoboes are men who have chosen to wander rather than work."

"Excuse me, Uncle Hendrick," Kit interrupted. She usually didn't say anything. But this time she had to speak up. "That's not true."

"I beg your pardon?" asked Uncle Hendrick icily.

"It's not true that all of the hoboes are men who have chosen to wander instead of working," Kit said. "Lots of them are on the road because they lost their jobs and their homes and they're trying to find work. And not all of the hoboes are men, either. Some are teenagers out on their own, some are women, and there are even whole families with little children."

Uncle Hendrick frowned at Kit. "Not another word out of you, Miss Impertinence," he said. "Write what I say. Keep your comments to yourself."

"Yes, sir," said Kit. She kept silent while Uncle Hendrick dictated the rest of his letter. But inside, she disagreed with every word.

"There!" said Uncle Hendrick, signing the letter. "Deliver this today."

Kit's heart sank as she took the letter. "But Uncle Hendrick," she protested. "I'm going to the airport with Dad and Charlie to take photos."

"No, you're not," said Uncle Hendrick, not the least bit sorry to be the bearer of bad news. "Mrs. Smithens came over earlier to tell your father that Mr. Hesse called. He doesn't want to drive anywhere because of the snow."

Kit looked out at the murky mid-morning sky. Snow was falling in a determined manner, as if it meant business. She sighed.

"Do as I say and deliver that letter," said Uncle Hendrick. "And do as I say and forget that nonsense you were blathering about earlier, too."

"It isn't nonsense," Kit insisted hotly, standing up to her uncle for once. "It's true. Hoboes are just poor people who are down on their luck."

"That," said Uncle Hendrick in a superior tone, "is just the kind of poppycock I'd expect your soft-headed parents to tell you."

It made Kit furious when Uncle Hendrick

34

criticized her parents. "No one told me that," she said. "I learned it myself. I've been to the hobo jungle and to a soup kitchen, too."

"Whatever for?" asked Uncle Hendrick. He looked at Kit with unconcealed horror. "Hoboes are thieves and beggars. Why go near them?"

"I want to help," Kit said simply. "Especially the children."

"Ha!" scoffed Uncle Hendrick so loudly that Kit jumped and Inky yipped. "You're nothing but a child yourself, still caught up in babyish play, like making newspapers! What help could *you* be?" He raised his eyebrows. "I suppose you're planning to end the Depression single-handedly, is that it?"

"No, of course not," Kit said, hating how Uncle Hendrick made her feel so foolish, flushed, and flustered. "I don't mean that. I know I can't change much by myself. Not me alone." She tried to settle her rattled thoughts and speak sensibly. "I just think that if people knew about the hobo children, if they saw how terrible the children's coats and shoes are, I'm sure they'd help," she said. "And then the children would know that people cared about them, and that would give them hope, and—"

"I suppose you're planning to end the Depression single-handedly, is that it?"

"Hope!" Uncle Hendrick cut in sharply. "An empty word. Comfort for fools. Hope never put a nickel in anybody's pocket, my girl, and hope is not going to end the Depression. Neither is pouring money into useless programs, or handing out coats or shoes to hobo children!" He dismissed Kit with a backward flutter of his hand, as if brushing away a tiresome fly. "Off with you," he said. "I, just like everyone else in the world, have better things to do than to listen to the jibber-jabber of a silly child like *you*. Go."

Kit left. She put Uncle Hendrick's letter in the laundry basket, wearily hoisted the basket onto her hip, then slowly trudged upstairs to her attic. Once there, she did not even have the energy to put her clothes away. Instead, she plunked down at her desk. Never had she felt so discouraged. Never had she felt such despair.

For almost two years, ever since Dad lost his job, she and her family had struggled through ups and downs, believing that if they worked hard enough, things would change for the better—not just for their family but for everyone hit hard by the Depression.

37

It was that hope that kept them going. If Uncle Hendrick was right, if hope was for fools, what did they have left? The Depression had won, and there was nothing anyone could do. There was certainly nothing *she* could do to change anything. Uncle Hendrick had made that clear to her.

Tears welled in Kit's eyes. She put one elbow on either side of her typewriter and held her head in her hands. She sniffed hard, trying not to cry. Then she took a deep, shaky breath. Somehow, the dark, inky smell of the typewriter ribbon just under her nose comforted her, and so did the solid, clunky black bulk of the typewriter itself. Next to the typewriter, Kit saw the drawing Stirling had made for their newspaper. He'd drawn her striding along, her camera slung around her neck, wearing her new coat. *Chipper*, she said to herself. *That is the perfect word to describe how I look in Stirling's drawing. And what would be the perfect word to describe how I feel now? Crushed? Flattened? No. Squashed.* Idly, Kit touched the **s** key. She remembered how Dad had fixed it when the typewriter was broken. He had repaired the typewriter for her because he knew how much writing meant to her. Kit pushed down hard on the **s** and the key struck the paper with a satisfying *whack*, a sound that Kit loved.

Kit sat bolt upright. Suddenly, she knew what she must do: write!

If Uncle Hendrick could write letters to the newspaper, she could, too. She might not be rich or important, but she knew how to write a letter that said what she wanted it to say. She'd deliver her letter right along with Uncle Hendrick's. It might not appear in the newspaper, it might not change anything or anyone else, but writing it would change the way she felt.

Quickly, Kit rolled the paper with the s on it out of the typewriter so she could write her rough draft on the back of it. She picked up her pencil. *Now*, she thought, *how should I begin?* Then Kit grinned. "To the Editor," she wrote. Wasn't that what Uncle Hendrick had taught her? Hadn't he, in fact, taught her exactly how to write a letter to the newspaper? How many times had he said that a letter must have one point to make and must make it in simple, direct language, using not more than two hundred and fifty words? Hadn't he told her over and over again that letters must be signed or they wouldn't be printed?

Without intending to, Uncle Hendrick had been a
very helpful teacher because of all his hectoring and
fusspot bossiness.

And Uncle Hendrick was not the only one
helping Kit. As she wrote, she thought of Dad's
dignity, Mother's industriousness, and the cheerful
good nature of the boarders. She thought of Charlie,
who'd come back from Montana with his "muscles
grown hard, back grown strong, and heart grown
stout," just as it said in the CCC booklet. She thought
of steadfast Stirling, funny Ruthie, and how kind and
neighborly Ruthie's family had been to hers. She
thought about thrifty, ingenious Aunt Millie, who
saved their house with her generosity; Will, the
young hobo who had taught her about courage; and
the little girl at the soup kitchen who'd brightened
with hope when Kit gave her the old coat. Thinking
about the way each one battled the Depression, its
losses and fears, gave strength to what Kit wrote.

Kit worked on her letter for a long time. She
chose her words carefully. She formed sentences in
her head, then wrote and rewrote them till they
sounded right. Then she read her rough draft aloud
to herself:

40

To the Editor:

*I think it is a good idea to use the hospital in
Covington as a home to house, feed, and clothe hoboes.
I have met some hoboes, and they are not all the same.
Every hobo has his or her own story. Some hoboes chose
a wandering life. Some people are hoboes because they lost
their jobs and their homes and have nowhere to go. Some
hoboes are grownups, some are young people, and there
are even hobo families with little children. Though they
all have different reasons for being on the road, I think
all hoboes hope the road they're on will lead them to better
times. But it is a long, hard trip, and they have nowhere
to stay on the way. I think they deserve our help,
sympathy, and compassion.*

*Hobo life is especially hard on children. They are
often hungry and cold. Their coats and shoes are worn-
out and outgrown. It would be a big help if people donated
coats and shoes for children to soup kitchens and missions.
It would show the children that we care about them, and
that would give them hope. It would give all of us hope,
too, because it would be a change for the better. Sometimes
hope is all any of us, hoboes or not, have to go on.*

*Margaret Mildred Kittredge
Cincinnati, Ohio*

Kit was pretty sure she had spelled *compassion* right. But something looked fishy about *sympathy*, and she didn't know whether *outgrown* was one word or two. Uncle Hendrick always said that there was no excuse for lazy spellers, and that a misspelled word made your reader lose confidence in you. So Kit looked up both *sympathy* and *outgrown* in the dictionary. When she was positive her spelling and punctuation were correct, she typed her letter very carefully. She struck every key hard, and with conviction. This time, Kit didn't care if the type-writer was noisy. Uncle Hendrick could hit the ceiling and Inky could howl and yowl. They were not going to stop her.

But there was no bluster or banging from below, and Kit was able to finish her letter in peace. She was folding it to put it into an envelope when Ruthie and Stirling came up the attic stairs.

"Hey, Kit," said Ruthie. "Want to come with Stirling and me? I've got some shoes and coats that're too small for me, and we're bringing them to the soup kitchen."

42

"Sure," said Kit. "Then after, I have some letters to deliver to the newspaper office."

"Letters with an 's'?" asked Stirling. "You mean Uncle Hendrick dictated two today?"

Kit smiled. "No," she said. "One is mine."

THE PERFECT
WORD

As they walked to the soup kitchen, Kit told Ruthie and Stirling about her argument with Uncle Hendrick and her decision to write a letter of her own. "I had to," she said. "Not just because I think he's wrong about the hoboes, but also because I felt so terrible when he said that hope was for fools."

"Well!" said Ruthie indignantly, her cheeks bright and her eyes snappy. "If you ask me, I think Uncle Hendrick is foolish *and* hopeless."

Snow was falling thick and fast. Enough had accumulated on the ground that the children kicked up cascades of it as they walked.

"Let's hurry," said Stirling. "It's getting slippery."

"I bet they'll have to call off school tomorrow," said Ruthie joyfully.

"Hurray!" cheered Kit and Stirling. "No school!" After that, the children didn't talk much. It was too hard to talk, because the wind was blowing the snow into their faces. Kit pulled her hat down over her ears and held her collar closed over her mouth. She bent forward, her shoulders hunched. The wind seemed to be coming from every direction at once. Sometimes it pushed against Kit as if trying to stop her. Then suddenly it would swoop around and push her from behind as if it were trying to hasten her along.

Kit thought it was a very good thing that she and Ruthie and Stirling knew the way to River Street so well. They had to walk with their eyes squinted shut against the stinging snow. Slowly they made their way to the alley behind the soup kitchen and up to its back door. They stopped to stomp the snow off their boots before they opened the door and went inside. The cooking area was busier than ever. And when the three children pushed through the big swinging door, they saw that the front room where the food was served was terribly crowded because of the harsh, wet weather.

"Oh, my," whispered Kit in dismay. The room smelled of wet wool. It seemed to Kit to be awash in a sea of gray, filled as it was with people wearing their snow-soaked winter coats and hats.

"I think," said Ruthie firmly, "we should give my old coats and shoes to someone in charge. I don't see how we'd choose who needs them most."

Kit agreed. The hobo children's coats and shoes were even worse than she remembered. They were so worn-out and filthy! They were such pitiful protection against the cold and wet of a day like today.

Stirling asked a woman serving food, and she pointed out the director of the soup kitchen. It took the three children a while to wriggle their way through the crowd to her. The room was so packed, it was hard not to jostle anyone or step on anyone's feet.

When they finally reached the director, Ruthie said, "Excuse me, ma'am. We brought these coats and shoes. We were hoping you'd give them to some children who need them."

"Why, thank you," said the director as she took the things from Ruthie. "I'll have no trouble finding new owners for these." She sighed. "Not many people think of the children. We have more and more children passing through here now, and all are in such desperate need."

After the director spoke, Kit remembered her own voice saying to Uncle Hendrick, *"If people knew about the hobo children . . ."* Kit slid her hand into her pocket to be sure her letter to the newspaper about the hobo children was safe. As she did, she felt something hard in her pocket. It was her camera. Again, she heard her own voice. This time it was saying, *"If they saw how terrible the children's coats and shoes are, I'm sure they'd help."*

Kit had an idea. Eagerly, she took her camera out of her pocket. "Would it be all right if we took some photographs of the children?" she asked the director.

"You must ask the children's permission and their parents', too," answered the director. "If they say yes, it's all right with me."

"Thanks!" said Kit. She and Ruthie and Stirling shared a quick grin. Kit did not even have to explain her brainstorm to her friends. They figured it out right away.

"We'll put the film in the envelope with your letter," said Ruthie.

"As I always say, a picture tells more about a person than words ever could," said Stirling.

Then they went into action. It was quite remarkable, Kit thought, how well they worked as a team. Without even talking about it, each one took a separate job. Ruthie asked the children if they'd like to have their pictures taken and explained politely to the parents what Kit wanted to do. Stirling told the children where to sit or stand and arranged their coats so that they'd show up clearly in the picture.

Kit worked the camera. She didn't have a flash, so she had to use light from the window. First she took pictures that showed the children from head to toe. Then she took pictures of the children's feet and makeshift shoes. Some children had taken their shoes off and lined them up to dry by a hissing radiator. Kit took a picture of the sad parade of shoes, which looked as exhausted as the children to whom they belonged. None of the shoes looked as if they could go another step.

Too soon, Kit had used all her film. "That's it,"

48

she said to Ruthie and Stirling. She put the film in the envelope with her letter. "Let's go."

The snowstorm was cruel and furious now. As Kit led Ruthie and Stirling to the newspaper offices, the children were blown and buffeted by the ice-cold wind. Every inch of the way was hard-won. It was a great relief to go inside the big brick building and be out of the swirling snow. It was very warm inside. Snow melted off the children's coats and boots and left a wet trail behind them as they climbed the stairs and walked through the newsroom to Gibb's desk.

Kit took the two letters out of her pocket, then hesitated. *Plip, plop.* The snow melting off her coat made an apologetic sound as it dripped to the floor. A small puddle formed around Kit's feet. Drops from her hat hit the letters.

"Put it in the box," ordered Gibb with even more impatience and less enthusiasm than usual. As always, he did not bother to look up.

Kit took a deep breath. She put the letter from Uncle Hendrick in the in-box. Under it she slid her own letter, which was bulgy with the roll of film and rather damp and wrinkled.

The three children left the newsroom and walked down the stairs. "Do you suppose they'll use the photos we took?" asked Stirling as the children paused to prepare themselves to face the storm before they went out of the newspaper office building.

"I don't know," Kit said.

"I wonder if they'll print your letter," mused Ruthie as she pulled on her mittens. "And if they do print it, do you think it'll change anything?"

"I don't know that, either," said Kit. She grinned crookedly. "Don't tell Uncle Hendrick, but I *hope* so."

The world was quiet, clean, and innocent under its fresh white layer of snow the next morning when Kit went out to walk Inky and buy Uncle Hendrick's newspaper. Uncle Hendrick always pitched a fit if his newspaper had been unfolded and read before he got it. So, even though she was bursting with curiosity, Kit knew she must not open up the paper to see if her letter and the photos had been printed. She had pretty much convinced herself that Gibb had tossed them in the trash. Still, it was hard not to feel optimistic on a beautiful morning like this, with the sun making a sparkling prism of every flake that caught its reflection.

Kit delivered the newspaper, his breakfast tray, and Inky to Uncle Hendrick. She fiddled awhile undoing the leash from Inky's collar, hoping that Uncle Hendrick would open up the newspaper and turn to the editorial page. But instead, Uncle Hendrick turned to her and said, "I don't want you now." So Kit had to leave.

She went downstairs and helped Mother serve breakfast to the boarders. They were all seated at the table when suddenly they heard Uncle Hendrick bellow and Inky yowl. Kit jumped up to go see what was the matter. But before she took a step, Uncle Hendrick exploded out of his room and came clomping down the stairs, with Inky yip-yapping close behind him. "What's the meaning of this?" Uncle Hendrick shouted, waving the newspaper over his head.

Kit sat down hard. *Could it be?* she wondered.

"Hello, Uncle Hendrick," said Mother, trying to calm him. "We are so pleased to see you back on your feet again!"

"Never mind," growled Uncle Hendrick. He slapped the newspaper onto the table, setting all the china rattling and making the silverware clink. Ignoring everyone else, he glared at Kit. "What have you done, young lady?"

Kit kicked Stirling under the table. They both tried to hide their smiles.

"I might have known you were in on it, too," Uncle Hendrick said to Stirling. "Young whippersnapper!"

"What is going on?" asked Dad. He picked up the newspaper and exclaimed, "Well, for heaven's sakes! There's a letter to the editor here from Kit. And there are photos with it, too!"

Pandemonium broke loose. Everyone jumped up from the table, all talking at once, and crowded around Dad to get a look at the newspaper. They didn't pay any attention to Uncle Hendrick, who was standing in the background making an angry speech to no one, pounding the floor with his cane, his remarks punctuated by Inky's barks. Grace, who loved mayhem, added her hoarse woofs to the hubbub, too.

"Settle down!" Dad called out. When everyone

was quiet, even Uncle Hendrick and Inky, Dad said, "I'm going to read Kit's letter aloud. I want everyone to listen."

Kit felt a warm blush begin at her toes and climb all the way up to the top of her head as Dad read her letter. Mother came and stood behind Kit's chair and put her hands on Kit's shoulders. When Dad had finished reading, she said, "Kit, I'm proud of you!" She leaned down and kissed Kit's cheek.

This was too much for Uncle Hendrick. "Proud?" he said, aghast. "Proud of that impudent girl?" He pointed an angry finger at Kit. "And you, a mere child, writing a letter to the newspaper! Where did you get such an idea?"

"Why, from you, of course, Uncle Hendrick," answered Kit politely.

Uncle Hendrick was speechless. A strange expression crossed his face. It seemed to be a mixture of annoyance and something that could have been respect. It lasted only a moment. Then Uncle Hendrick turned away and stalked off, Inky trailing behind him.

After that, everyone congratulated Kit, and Stirling, too. But Kit barely heard them. She held

the newspaper in her two hands and looked at her letter and the photographs. Thousands of people would read this newspaper and see the photos. Thousands of people would read words that *she* had written. Kit shivered with delight. She could hardly believe it was true.

Ruthie was right. School *was* closed that day because of the snow. In fact, school was closed for a week after the storm, which turned out to have been the worst blizzard to hit Cincinnati in years.

So it was more than a week later, at the end of the first day back, that Kit, Ruthie, and Stirling found themselves walking to the soup kitchen after school. Lots of Kit's classmates had read her letter and seen the photos in the newspaper. They had brought their old coats and shoes to school. Some of Kit and Stirling's egg customers had also seen the letter and the photos, and they had made donations of clothing, too. Kit and Stirling were staggering under armloads of coats, and Ruthie was pulling the wagon, which was full of boots and shoes. They

*Thousands of people would read words that **she** had written. Kit shivered with delight. She could hardly believe it was true.*

55

brought their donations straight to the director of the soup kitchen.

The director smiled broadly at them. "I am so glad to see the three of you!" she said. "You're the children who took the photos, aren't you?"

Kit, Ruthie, and Stirling nodded.

The director asked Kit, "And are you the one who wrote the letter?"

"Yes, ma'am," said Kit.

"We've had many more donations for the children since your letter and those photos appeared in the newspaper," said the director. "You drew attention to a real need. You three have truly made a difference. Thank you."

"You're welcome," said Kit, Ruthie, and Stirling, beaming.

As it happened, Kit had another letter of Uncle Hendrick's to deliver to the newspaper office. This one was about Eleanor Roosevelt. Uncle Hendrick highly disapproved of the work she was doing to help miners in West Virginia. The letter was so full of fiery words that Kit was surprised it wasn't hot to the touch.

This time, it was a quick, easy walk to the newspaper building, since the weather was clear. Upstairs, the newsroom was just as noisy and busy as ever, and Gibb was as distracted as always when the children came to his desk. Kit started to put Uncle Hendrick's letter in Gibb's in-box.

"Hold on," said Gibb.

Kit stopped.

Gibb tilted his head toward the letter. "Is that one of his or one of yours?" he asked.

"His," Kit answered.

"Put it in the box," said Gibb in his usual brusque way. Then his voice changed. "But any time you've got something else *you* want to write, bring it here. You've got the makings of a good reporter, kid."

Kit was so happy she could hardly speak. "Thanks," she said. Out of the corner of her eye, she saw Ruthie and Stirling nudge each other and grin.

The three of them walked home together along the slushy sidewalks, dodging puddles of melted snow. But the sky was blue overhead, and there was a certain softness in the air that seemed to Kit to carry the scent of spring. It was just a hint, just a whiff, but it was full of promise.

That's it, thought Kit. *That's the perfect word. I feel full of* **promise**.

Looking
Back
1934

A PEEK INTO
THE PAST

Waiting for job interviews at an employment agency

Kit's story ends in 1934, but the Great Depression continued until the early 1940s. By 1934, many American families were in the same position as the Kittredges. They had found ways to make ends meet in spite of lost jobs and lost hopes, but times were still hard and they had no idea when the Depression might end. Everyone did whatever was necessary to survive and hoped that the newly elected president could find a way to end the Depression.

These girls helped their school save money by cleaning up the school themselves.

Lines of worried people waiting to withdraw money from banks was a common sight before FDR's "bank holiday."

President Franklin Delano Roosevelt knew he needed to act fast to fight the Depression. One of the first official acts during his first one hundred days in office dealt with the banks. By 1933, thousands of banks had run out of money and closed, taking many people's life savings with them. People got scared when they heard about bank closings. They rushed to take all their money out of their local banks, which created even more problems—and sometimes caused banks to fail completely.

To stop more banks from failing, Roosevelt declared a "bank holiday" and temporarily closed all banks. He then went on the radio and told the public exactly what he was doing. He explained to people that their money would be safe because the government would *insure* their accounts. Under his new plan, if a bank failed and couldn't pay its customers, the government promised to step in and make sure the depositors got their money back. Americans were reassured by Roosevelt's words, and took their money back to the banks.

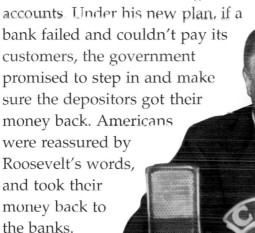

Roosevelt's radio address about America's banks was the first of many radio "fireside chats" broadcast to the American people.

Along with bold action to stabilize the banks, President Roosevelt created relief and jobs programs as part of the "new deal" he had promised Americans during the election. With the help of business leaders, Roosevelt and the National Recovery Administration (NRA) set minimum wages and maximum hours for workers, so workers earned a higher hourly wage and jobs could be spread among as many workers as possible. People were encouraged to buy products made under the NRA, and the NRA blue eagle began to be used as a show of support for the program.

Some New Deal programs didn't last long. The Civil Works Administration (CWA) created part-time jobs for older men, such as Kit's dad, but it lasted only a few months.

These Hollywood starlets showed their support by having the NRA eagle suntanned on their backs!

WPA artists worked on projects ranging from huge painted murals to posters to hand-carved puppets.

The Works Progress Administration (WPA) replaced the CWA in early 1935, and it *was* successful. Public buildings still in use today were built under this program, and many included murals and art created by WPA artists. Other programs, such as the Federal Writers' Project, the Federal Music Program, and the Federal Theater Project, provided jobs to writers, musicians, and actors.

One of Roosevelt's most enduring New Deal programs—and one still in effect today—was the Social Security Administration. It provided for and protected retirement funds for American workers.

The first Social Security cards were issued in December 1936.

Social Security assigned a number to all workers in order to keep track of their retirement funds, but some people didn't like being identified by a number.

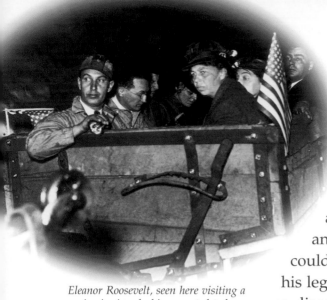

Eleanor Roosevelt, seen here visiting a mine in Appalachia, reported to her husband everything she saw in her travels.

Eleanor Roosevelt was one of the most active First Ladies ever. She considered herself to be the eyes and ears of the President, and she went places he could not easily go, because his legs were paralyzed by a disease called *polio*. Many Americans, grateful for her public presence and her concern for people in need, grew to respect and love Mrs. Roosevelt.

However, like Kit's Uncle Hendrick, other Americans detested both Franklin and Eleanor Roosevelt. People like Uncle Hendrick believed that the New Deal programs were bad for America and did not like what they thought of as government "meddling" in business and in private citizens' lives.

In spite of the Roosevelts' efforts, the Depression continued through the 1930s. Things improved slightly—and slowly—as America tried to climb out of the slippery hole of the Depression. Temporary jobs were created, but when funds

Children suffered from hunger and lack of adequate clothing when their parents didn't have jobs.

Dust storms blew huge clouds of dust and dirt across the Midwest and the South.

ran out and unemployment rose again in a *recession*, the country's economy started slipping back into the hole of the Depression. During the 1937 recession, FDR reported grimly, "I see one-third of a nation ill-housed, ill-clad, ill-nourished," as he continued to search for solutions to America's problems.

Among the lowest points were the great dust storms in the Midwest. Careless farming practices and prolonged *drought,* or dry spells, caused rich topsoil to dry up and blow away in huge gray and brown clouds. Hundreds of thousands of families lost their farms and went west to California, where they did temporary farmwork and lived under miserable conditions in migrant camps.

Migrant children often took care of their younger sisters and brothers while their parents worked in the fields.

The Depression finally ended, in part because of another crisis, one that had been brewing overseas for years. In the 1920s and 1930s, a German leader named Adolf Hitler had been gaining power. Germany had

*Adolf Hitler salutes his followers, who were known as **Nazis**.*

suffered its own depression after losing World War One in 1918, and Hitler promised the German people a return to prosperity if they followed him.

Hitler also rebuilt the German army and started invading other European countries. He formed partner-ships with Italy in Europe and with Japan in the Pacific. In addition, Hitler *persecuted* certain groups, or treated them harshly and unfairly. Among those groups were Jewish people, Gypsies, Jehovah's Witnesses, and others whose politics and lifestyles he did not agree with. Americans were concerned about Hitler's increasing power, but most did not want to fight in another war overseas. Instead, America helped its *allies*, its friends who were fighting Germany, by producing war supplies.

Factories geared up to produce war goods to fight Germany.

Japanese pilots took this photo of their attack on the U.S. Army base next to Pearl Harbor. After the attack, America declared war.

The New York Times.
U.S. DECLARES WAR, PACIFIC BATTLE WIDENS; MANILA AREA BOMBED; 1,500 DEAD IN HAWAII: HOSTILE PLANES SIGHTED AT SAN FRANCISCO

BOMBERS RAID MANILA

U. S. DECLARES WAR ON JAPAN

The new factory jobs created to produce war supplies for America's allies helped end the Depression in the United States. Americans were happy to have a growing economy again, but most still did not want to go to war. However, in December 1941, Japan attacked the United States by bombing the Hawaiian port of Pearl Harbor, and America entered the war.

Kit would have been 18 years old when America entered World War Two. She might have become a nurse or a factory worker. Or, with her talent for writing, Kit

might have become a war correspondent, covering the war and writing stories about what she saw. The same resourcefulness, hard work, cooperation, and compassion that got Kit and other Americans through the Depression were what they relied on to get through the war years. By the time the Great Depression and World War Two ended, Americans were ready for peace, prosperity, and stability.

A World War Two war correspondent

At the war's end, families gathered to celebrate peace and the return to prosperity.

THE BOOKS ABOUT KIT

MEET KIT • An American Girl
Kit Kittredge and her family get news that
turns their household upside down.

KIT LEARNS A LESSON • A School Story
It's Thanksgiving, and Kit learns a surprising
lesson about being thankful.

KIT'S SURPRISE • A Christmas Story
The Kittredges may lose their house.
Can Kit still find a way to make Christmas
merry and bright for her family?

HAPPY BIRTHDAY, KIT! • A Springtime Story
Kit loves Aunt Millie's thrifty ideas—until Aunt Millie
plans a pinch-penny party and invites Kit's whole class.

KIT SAVES THE DAY • A Summer Story
Kit's curiosity and longing for adventure
lead her to unexpected places—and into trouble!

CHANGES FOR KIT • A Winter Story
Kit writes a letter that brings changes and
new hope—in spite of the hard times.

◆

WELCOME TO KIT'S WORLD • 1934
American history is lavishly portrayed
with photographs, illustrations, and
excerpts from real girls' letters and diaries.

MORE TO DISCOVER! While books are the heart of
The American Girls Collection,® they are only the beginning. The stories  in the Collection come to life when you act them out with the beautiful American Girls dolls and their exquisite clothes and accessories. To request a free catalogue full of things girls love, send in this postcard, call **1-800-845-0005,** or visit our Web site at **americangirl.com**.

Please send me an American Girl®catalogue.

My name is _____

My address is _____

City _____ State _____ Zip _____
1961i

My birth date is ____/____/____ E-mail address _____
 month   day   year Fill in to receive updates and web exclusive offers.

Parent's signature _____

And send a catalogue to my friend.

My friend's name is _____

Address _____

City _____ State _____ Zip _____
1225i

If the postcard has already been removed from this book and you would like to receive an American Girl® catalogue, please send your name and address to:

American Girl
P.O. Box 620497
Middleton, WI 53562-0497

You may also call our toll-free number, **1-800-845-0005,** or visit our Web site at **americangirl.com**.

Place
Stamp
Here

PO BOX 620497
MIDDLETON WI 53562-0497

|ı|lı.ıll.ılıl.ıllıı.ılıllllıı.lıılllıIıılıı.ıllılıılıılıllı|